REDUCE, REUSE, RECYCLE

BY ELIZABETH THOMAS

Published by The Child's World®
1980 Lookout Drive • Mankato, MN 56003-1705
800-599-READ • www.childsworld.com

PHOTO CREDITS
Carrie Bottomley/iStockphoto, cover, 1; Shutterstock Images, 5, 17, 29;
Mark Sayer/Shutterstock Images, 7; Fotolia, 9; Elena Elisseeva/
Shutterstock Images, 11; Paul Turner/Shutterstock Images, 13; Paul
Prescott/Shutterstock Images, 15; Mario Aguilar/Shutterstock Images, 19;
Julián Rovagnati/Shutterstock Images, 21; Hank Frentz/Fotolia, 23;
Evgenia Bolyukh/Shutterstock Images, 25; Robyn Mackenzie/
Shutterstock Images, 27

CONTENT CONSULTANT
Jacques Finlay, Associate Professor, Department of Ecology,
Evolution and Behavior, University of Minnesota

ACKNOWLEDGMENTS
The Child's World®: Mary Berendes, Publishing Director
The Design Lab: Design
Red Line Editorial: Editorial direction

ISBN: 978-1-60973-176-2
LCCN: 2011927675

Printed in the United States of America in Mankato, MN
July, 2011
PA02090

TABLE OF CONTENTS

THE THREE Rs

You want to help keep Earth beautiful and clean. What can you do? Just remember the three Rs: **reduce**, **reuse**, and **recycle**. These are some of the easiest ways you can cut back on waste and help keep the environment clean. But what do they mean?

To *reduce* means to use less. We can reduce the amount of garbage we throw away. That way, less will go into landfills. There will be more room for nature, animals, and people. In general, it's always best to buy and use less than to have to throw away extras or leftovers.

To *reuse* means to use again. You can change used clothes, dishes, toys, and other items into different, useful things.

By reducing, reusing, and recycling, you help cut back on waste. This helps keep Earth clean.

You can sew holes, tape tears, glue cracks, reuse screws and nails, and fix all kinds of broken things. You don't have to throw away the things you no longer want. You can donate or sell your used items.

To *recycle* means to dispose of things so they can be used for a similar or different purpose. Look for the recycling logo to see if something can be recycled.

REDUCE: SHORTEN YOUR SHOWER TIME

The average 10- to 15-minute shower uses about 25 to 35 gallons (95–132 L) of water. Think of that as about 35 big milk jugs full of water! By taking a quick, five-minute shower, you'll save water and the energy it takes to heat it. You'll save time, too!

WHY?

Showers use a lot of water. About 20 percent of water used indoors is used for showers. By taking shorter showers, you'll reduce how much indoor water you use.

A running shower uses many gallons of water. Take quicker, more efficient showers to save water and time!

REDUCE: LESS TOILET WATER

There are easy ways to use less water in your toilet. Find two 16-ounce (473 mL) plastic bottles with screw-on caps. Pour an inch or two (2.5–5.1 cm) of sand into the bottles. Fill them up with water. Have a grown-up help you take the top off the toilet tank. Place the bottles inside the tank, away from the flushing parts. Put the lid back on the tank.

WHY?

It takes between 1.6 and 3.5 gallons (6.1–13.2 L) of water to flush the toilet. The bottles in the tank will take up space, so less water will be needed to fill up the tank. This simple step will reduce the amount of water used with each flush!

Placing plastic bottles in the toilet tank reduces the amount of water needed to fill up the tank after flushing.

9

REDUCE: FLIP THE SWITCH

Use less energy by always turning off the lights when you leave a room. Soon, it will become an energy-saving habit. Remember to turn off your computer when it is not being used, too! It does not use as much energy as other things in the house, but it still uses energy—even when it is "sleeping."

WHY?

Most electricity in the United States is made by power plants that burn coal. This pollutes the air and contributes to **global warming**. Someday, all electricity may be made by the sun, wind, and other ways that do not harm Earth. Until then, keep flipping that switch!

Save energy by turning off the lights when you leave a room.

TIP #4

REUSE: WRAP WITH THE FUNNIES

Giving presents is great. It's even greater when you can do it while reusing old paper and reducing waste. The next time you have to wrap a present, get creative! Think of ways to wrap it without buying fancy wrapping paper. Use the comics from yesterday's newspaper. Use a brown paper bag and decorate it with drawings, stickers, or pictures. Use scraps of leftover fabric. Use what's in the house and make the most of using less.

WHY?

Throughout the world, about 4 billion trees are used in paper industries each year. Wrapping paper is one of the items made from trees. By not buying wrapping paper, you can help reduce the number of trees that are cut down every year.

Reuse old newspaper as wrapping paper. This reduces paper waste and makes a gift unique.

YOU'RE NEVER TOO YOUNG TO START!

When Alec Loorz was 12, he saw the film *An Inconvenient Truth*. The movie is about global warming and what can be done to prevent it. He asked to be trained as a presenter for the Climate Project, but he was turned down because he was too young. Alec created his own presentation about global warming and gave it more than 30 times before the Climate Project managers changed their minds. They made him the youngest presenter with the project. Alec has also started his own organization, Kids vs. Global Warming.

REUSE: MAKE A PLANTER

Yogurt cups and other plastic containers can be pots for plants. Wash and dry an empty yogurt cup. Punch a few holes in the bottom. Place it on the lid. Fill the cup three-fourths full with soil from the garden. Push the seed into the soil and water it. The lid will catch any excess water. When the seedlings get bigger, plant them outside in the garden. Then recycle the container!

WHY?

Plastics that end up in landfills take a long time to break down. The fewer plastic items we put in our landfills, the longer it will take to fill up the landfills. Because plants breathe in carbon dioxide, growing a garden from seedlings is a wonderful way to help clean the air and get fresh fruit and vegetables.

Help cut back on the amount of plastic waste. Reuse plastic containers as planters by filling them with soil and seeds.

REUSE: CLOTHING EXCHANGE

There are many ways to reuse clothing. Before you go shopping for new clothes, invite your friends over for a clothing exchange. Each person brings some clothes he or she doesn't wear anymore. Enjoy sharing them with each other. Invent one-of-a-kind looks. You can donate any remaining items to a charity.

WHY?

Each year, Americans throw away around 6 million tons (5 million t) of clothes and footwear! All those clothes are filling up our landfills very quickly. Those items could be going to people in need.

A clothing exchange is a great way to update your wardrobe and help Earth.

REDUCE: BRING YOUR OWN BAG

Here's a great way to reduce waste. Next time your family goes shopping, bring your own bag. A cloth bag can be used over and over again. When it gets dirty, just wash it.

WHY?

Bringing your own bag means one less plastic bag needs to be made from petroleum, which causes many problems. These include water and air pollution and global warming.

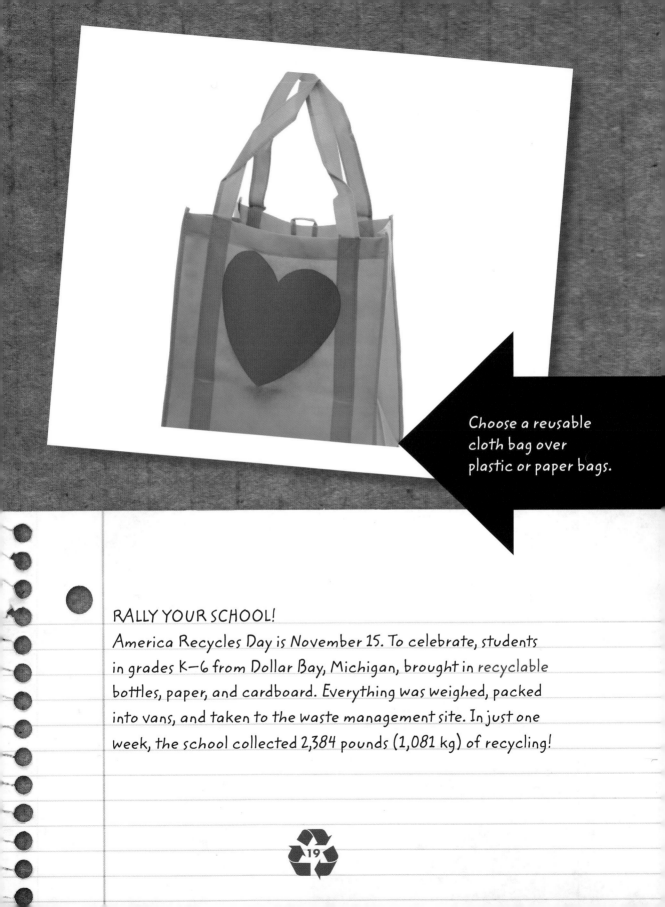

Choose a reusable cloth bag over plastic or paper bags.

RALLY YOUR SCHOOL!

America Recycles Day is November 15. To celebrate, students in grades K–6 from Dollar Bay, Michigan, brought in recyclable bottles, paper, and cardboard. Everything was weighed, packed into vans, and taken to the waste management site. In just one week, the school collected 2,384 pounds (1,081 kg) of recycling!

REDUCE: RIDE YOUR BIKE

You might not have your driver's license yet, but you can still help save gas. Instead of asking for a ride to your friend's house, ride your bike. Instead of getting a ride to soccer practice, ride your bike. Use your bike for as many trips as you can.

WHY?

You'll help reduce the amount of pollution put in the air. Gasoline and diesel fuel exhaust from vehicles are a major source of carbon dioxide. This is a **greenhouse gas** that traps heat in Earth's atmosphere. Too much greenhouse gas in the atmosphere causes global warming.

Ride your bike or walk whenever and wherever you can instead of getting a ride in a car.

REDUCE: PRECYCLE

Think before you buy! **Precycling** is a way to make sure the things you buy are recyclable. Before you buy anything new—a shirt or a juice—check to make sure it can be recycled. If the shirt is made of natural fibers—like 100 percent cotton—it will break down faster in a landfill when it wears out and has to be thrown away. If you buy a juice, make sure that the bottle is recyclable.

WHY?

When you shop, you are "voting" with your dollars. You want to vote for companies that care about the environment. Precycling lets you do that.

Try to reduce the number of items you use that cannot be recycled.

REUSE: BRING CONTAINERS

If you bring your lunch to school, bring a reusable lunch bag instead of a paper sack. Get a set of reusable plastic containers to keep your food in. You can even reuse plastic bags. Just wash them and let them dry.

WHY?

Each person in the United States uses one Douglas fir 100 feet (30 m) tall in paper and wood products per year! Reducing the number of paper bags you use means fewer trees are cut down. These trees provide oxygen and absorb carbon dioxide in the air. In other words, more trees mean more oxygen and less global warming!

Pack your lunch in
reusable containers
to reduce waste.

REDUCE: CLOTH, NOT PAPER

Start using cloth napkins for your family dinners. You can begin by using cloth napkins one night per week and then use them more frequently. Soon, you'll have no paper napkin waste after a meal. Cloth napkins feel softer on your mouth and hands, too.

WHY?

In an average year, each American uses about 2,200 paper napkins. That's about six a day! If everyone in the United States used just one less paper napkin a day, more than half a million tons (454,000 t) of napkins could be saved from landfills every year.

26

Reduce paper waste
by using cloth napkins
at the dinner table.

27

TIP #12

RECYCLE: CRAYON COLLECTION

Start a recycling program in your classroom or school. You can recycle old and broken crayons by sending them to a crayon recycling company. The company will melt down the crayons into fun, new shapes! Or, with the help of adult, you can melt down your old crayons into an art project.

WHY?

It takes less energy to recycle materials into new things than to make the things from scratch. Less energy used in factories means less global warming.

Old crayons can be recycled into new ones.

IT PAYS TO RECYCLE!

The students at Deibler Elementary School in Perkasie, Pennsylvania, have found a fun way to recycle and earn money at the same time! On Earth Day in 2009, the third grade class started to recycle juice pouches. The pouches were turned into backpacks and homework folders, among other things. The students were paid two cents a pouch. As of December 2010, they had raised over $770! The money has been used for class trips, assemblies, and family fun nights.

MORE WAYS TO GO GREEN

1. **Borrow** a book, game, or CD from the library instead of buying one.

2. **Refill** glass or plastic bottles with water and take them with you on the go.

3. **Use** refillable pens and pencils.

4. **Use** rechargeable batteries.

5. **Buy** items from a secondhand store. Clothes, shoes, and toys are usually in good condition. The store might buy them back from you when you outgrow them, too.

6. **Turn** off the water while you brush your teeth.

7. **Use** empty coffee cans to hold crayons, pens, or coins.

8. **Don't** ever litter!

9. **Instead** of turning up the heat, put on a sweater.

10. **Volunteer** to organize a cleanup of your school, neighborhood, park, or town.

11. **Make** sure your family recycles old phonebooks.

12. **Help** organize a carpool with your friends and their parents.

13. **Plant** a tree.

14. **Eat** less fast food! Fast food uses a lot of packaging that will end up in a landfill.

WORDS TO KNOW

global warming (GLOHB-ul WOR-ming): Global warming is the heating up of Earth's atmosphere and oceans due to air pollution. You can help stop global warming by reducing, reusing, and recycling.

greenhouse gas (GREEN-houss GASS): A greenhouse gas is a gas like carbon dioxide or methane that helps hold heat in the atmosphere. Too much greenhouse gas in the atmosphere contributes to global warming.

precycling (PREE-sy-kul-ing): Precycling means making sure things can be recycled before buying them. Precycling reduces waste that goes into landfills.

recyclable (ree-SY-kluh-bul): If something is recyclable, it can be recycled. Glass bottles and aluminum cans are recyclable.

recycle (ree-SY-kul): To recycle means to convert waste into reusable material. You can recycle soda cans, newspapers, and more.

reduce (ree-DOOS): To reduce means to make smaller or less in amount or size. If you reduce waste, you make less garbage.

reuse (ree-YOOZ): To reuse means to use more than once. It is a good idea to reuse clothes, toys, and other items.

FURTHER READING

BOOKS

Ostopowish, Melanie. *Refuse, Misuse, and Reuse.* Chicago: Raintree, 2004.

Ross, Kathy. *Earth-Friendly Crafts: Clever Ways to Reuse Everyday Items.* Minneapolis, MN: Millbrook Press, 2009.

Rutty, Gregory. *Help Your Parents Save the Planet: 50 Simple Ways to Go Green Now!* New York: Play Bac Publishing, 2009.

WEB SITES

Visit our Web site for links about reducing, reusing, and recycling:
http://www.childsworld.com/links

Note to Parents, Teachers, and Librarians: We routinely verify our Web links to make sure they are safe and active sites. So encourage your readers to check them out!

INDEX